TULSA CITY-COUNTY LIBRARY

S0-BDG-419

Bat and Sloth
Lost and Found

Time to Read™ is an early reader program designed to guide children to literacy success regardless of age or grade level. The program's three levels correspond to stages of reading readiness, making book selection straightforward, and assuring that when it's time for a child to read, the right book is waiting.

| — Level — 1 | **Beginning to Read** | • Large, simple type | • Word repetition |
| | | • Basic vocabulary | • Strong illustration support |

| — Level — 2 | **Reading with Help** | • Short sentences | • Simple dialogue |
| | | • Engaging stories | • Illustration support |

| — Level — 3 | **Reading Independently** | • Longer sentences | • Short paragraphs |
| | | • Harder words | • Increased story complexity |

To Meg, a friend found,
and then found again.
LK

To Joey
SB

Library of Congress Cataloging-in-Publication data
is on file with the publisher.

Text copyright © 2020 by Leslie Kimmelman
Illustrations copyright © 2020 by Albert Whitman & Company
Illustrations by Seb Braun
First published in the United States of America in 2020
by Albert Whitman & Company
ISBN 978-0-8075-0586-1 (hardcover)
ISBN 978-0-8075-0588-5 (ebook)
All rights reserved. No part of this book may be reproduced or transmitted
in any form or by any means, electronic or mechanical, including
photocopying, recording, or by any information storage and retrieval system,
without permission in writing from the publisher.

Printed in China
10 9 8 7 6 5 4 3 2 1 WKT 24 23 22 21 20 19

Design by Rick DeMonico

For more information about Albert Whitman & Company,
visit our website at www.albertwhitman.com.

Bat and Sloth
Lost and Found

Leslie Kimmelman

illustrated by
Seb Braun

Albert Whitman & Company
Chicago, Illinois

Lost!

The night was over.
It was almost bedtime.
Bat had flown far.

He had loop-de-looped.
He had flown higher than
any bat had ever flown.
("I'm *pretty* sure," he said.)

He had seen the stars twinkle.
He had seen the moon wink.
"I can't wait to tell
my friend, Sloth," he said.
So Bat headed home.

There were trees in every direction.
But Bat was not worried.
He knew which tree was his.
He knew which branch was his.
Zip! He dove down.
Nope. Wrong tree.

Bat rose back up.

He flew in wide circles, looking.

"Oh, there it is," he said.

Zip! He dove down again.

"That is not my tree either,"

Bat said, starting to worry.

"My tree smells just so.
My tree looks just so.
And my tree has Sloth."
Zip! Dive.
Zip! Dive.
Zip! Dive.

Bat kept looking for the right tree
and the right branch.
Bat kept finding the wrong trees
and the wrong branches.
"WHERE IS MY TREE?" cried Bat.
"WHERE IS SLOTH?"
Bat was lost.

Also Lost

Sloth went for a moonlight swim.
The water was cool and fine.
He swam fast.
"Bat would be surprised
that I am so speedy,"
he said to himself.
"Bat zips through the sky,
but I zip through the water."

Zip! Zip! Splash!
Finally Sloth got out of the water.
The moon was sinking.
The stars were gone.
It was bedtime.

Out of the water, Sloth did not zip.
Sloth S-L-O-W-L-Y crawled to his tree.
He S-L-O-W-L-Y crawled to his branch.
Well, not *his* tree. Not *his* branch.
"*Our* branch," said Sloth to himself,
thinking of his friend, Bat.

But Bat was not there.

The sun was coming up,
and Bat was not there.
BAT WAS NOT THERE?
When it was time to sleep
after a long night,
Bat was always there.

"BAT! WHERE ARE YOU?"
Sloth shouted.
He knew that Bat would answer.
Bat loved to talk.
But there was no answer.
"BAT!" shouted Sloth. "COME HOME!
I AM LOST WITHOUT YOU!"

A New Friend

Sloth was lonely.
This is not a one-animal branch,
he thought. This branch was made for two.
Did the branch hear him?
Suddenly it moved.

"BAT!" cried Sloth.

But it was not Bat.

"Who are you?" asked Sloth.

"Kinkajou," answered the kinkajou.

"Can I please share your branch?"

"Um," said Sloth.

"Um?" Kinkajou repeated.

"Um," said Sloth again.

"This is Bat's branch, too.
You can share with us both."

"A bat?" said Kinkajou.

She made a face.

"Why are you friends with a bat?"

"Why not?" Sloth replied.

"Bats are nothing like us,"
said Kinkajou.
"Not true," said Sloth.
"Bat is a mammal, like us.
Bat eats fruit, like us.
Bat likes the night, like we do."

"I guess so," said Kinkajou.
"But he has wings
and only a little bit of fur."
"So?" replied Sloth slowly.
"He is my friend.
He will be here soon."

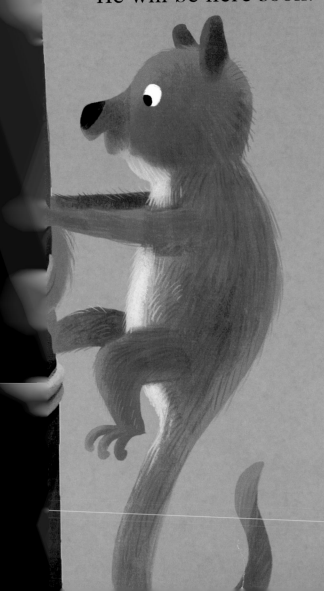

Kinkajou looked at Sloth.
"I have never met a bat before," she said.
"But if *you* are friends with Bat,
then *I* am friends with Bat."

Kinkajou gave Sloth a fig.
As he chewed,
she picked bugs off his fur.
Then Sloth and Kinkajou waited,
upside down, for Bat to come home.

Found!

Bat did not come home.

"Hey Sloth?" Kinkajou said finally.

"I think your friend may need our help."

"Yes," agreed Sloth. "I think so."

Sloth squealed and screamed.
Kinkajou hissed and shrieked.
They were LOUD!

Suddenly there was a *whoosh*!

"BAT!" cried Sloth.

"SLOTH!" cried Bat.

"KINKAJOU!" cried Kinkajou.

"Who are you?" asked Bat.

"Kinkajou," repeated Kinkajou.
"I am Sloth's friend.
And if you are Sloth's friend,
then I am your friend, too."

"Why did you move our tree?"
Bat asked Sloth.
"I couldn't find my way home.
Then I heard you."

"Trees don't move," Kinkajou giggled.

"No," agreed Sloth.

"Hmm," said Bat, thinking.

"I did a giant loop-de-loop,"
he told Sloth and Kinkajou.

"That must be when I lost my way."

"But you're here now,"
Sloth told his friend.
"That's what matters."
Bat made up a little tune.
"Me, you, Kinkajou, too,
just us three, on our tree."

And as the sun's rays
shone through the rain forest,
Bat, Sloth, and Kinkajou
settled in for a good day's sleep.